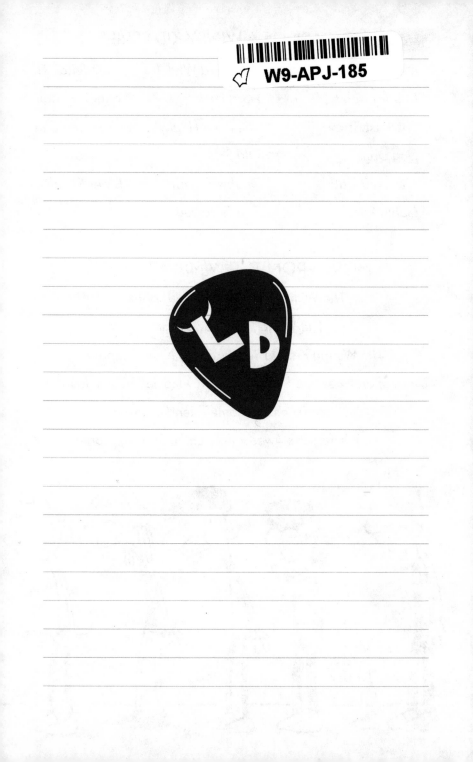

THE *DIARY OF A WIMPY KID* SERIES

MORE FROM THE *WIMPY* WORLD

DIARY
of a
Wimpy Kid

DIPER
ÖVERLÖDE

by Jeff Kinney

AMULET BOOKS

New York

Cataloging-in-Publication Data has been applied for and may be obtained from the Library of Congress.

Paperback ISBN 978-1-4197-6651-0

Book design by Jeff Kinney
Cover design by Jeff Kinney with Pamela Notarantonio and Lora Grisafi

"Can You Smell Us Now?"
Lyrics by Jeff Kinney, music by Jon Levine.
© 2022 Fox Film Music Corp., Primary Wave Music (BMI)
All Rights Reserved. Used with Permission.

Published in 2022 by Amulet Books, an imprint of ABRAMS. All rights reserved. No portion of this book may be reproduced, stored in a retrieval system, or transmitted in any form or by any means, mechanical, electronic, photocopying, recording, or otherwise, without written permission from the publisher.

Printed and bound in U.S.A.
10 9 8 7 6 5 4 3 2 1

Amulet Books are available at special discounts when purchased in quantity for premiums and promotions as well as fundraising or educational use. Special editions can also be created to specification. For details, contact specialsales@abramsbooks.com or the address below.

Amulet Books® is a registered trademark of Harry N. Abrams, Inc.

ABRAMS The Art of Books
195 Broadway, New York, NY 10007
abramsbooks.com

TO SCOTT

Monday

I always thought I wanted to be rich and famous, but now I'm starting to wonder if fame and fortune are worth all the hassle.

I'm sure it would be great to be a celebrity, because it'd be nice to get the rock star treatment and see your name in lights.

But there's only so much attention one person can take, and I bet that kind of thing would get kind of old after a while.

If you're famous, you can't just turn it off whenever it's inconvenient. And it wouldn't be much fun getting mobbed for autographs and selfies all the time.

When you're a celebrity, you can't even take care of your personal business without everyone finding out and posting about it on social media.

And when you're out in public, someone's bound to snap a picture of you when you're not looking your best.

On top of that, everyone feels like they have the right to know all the details about your personal relationships, which can't be a lot of fun, either.

3

Speaking of relationships, when you're a celebrity, you never know who you can TRUST. Because even the people closest to you will be happy to air your dirty laundry if the price is right.

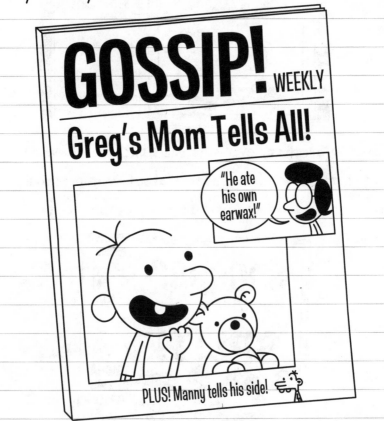

The celebrities who have it the WORST are former child stars, because after they grow up and fall out of the spotlight, they have to learn how to live like regular people.

And I'm sure it's no fun being someone who USED to be famous.

People recognize former child stars even after they've become adults. And I'd like to be able to enjoy a meal with my family in public without getting hassled by fans later on.

Don't get me wrong, it would be nice to have mansions and expensive cars and all the other stuff that comes with being famous. I just wouldn't want to deal with the downside of fame.

That's why it would be awesome to be FRIENDS with someone who's famous. Then you'd get all the perks of being a celebrity without any of the negatives.

Famous people are always traveling the world and going on fancy vacations. And I could definitely see myself getting used to that kind of lifestyle, especially if I wasn't the one paying.

AHHH!

Plus, if you're friends with someone who has more money than you, you can always count on them to pick up the tab.

DOES THIS STEAK LOOK MEDIUM RARE TO YOU?

And if you and your famous friend ever have a falling-out, it wouldn't be the end of the world. Because people will pay good money for juicy celebrity gossip.

GOSSIP! WEEKLY
Greg Heffley Spills!

"He's a bad tipper!"

CHEAPSKATE
Rowley Jefferson

The only problem with my plan is that I don't have any friends who are on track to become famous. And even though I've tried to encourage my friend Rowley to start making a name for himself, he just doesn't seem all that interested.

THE Amazing Rowley HUMAN CANNONBALL

So I've decided that what would be even better than being friends with a celebrity is being RELATED to one. Because you know your Christmas presents are gonna be WAY nicer if you've got a rich person in the family.

My older brother, Rodrick, actually has big plans to become a famous musician.

But I just don't know how realistic it is to be successful when your band's name is Löded Diper.

Aside from their name, Löded Diper has a few obstacles standing in their way. The first one is that they still practice in our basement, even though my parents probably wish they DIDN'T.

On top of that, Löded Diper hasn't played an actual show in more than a year. And the only member of the band who's not in high school is the lead singer, Bill. But he's thirty-five years old and lives in his gramma's basement.

Even with all that, Rodrick still thinks Löded Diper can make it to the big time. And he's come up with a plan for how they can do it.

There's a competition called the Battle of the Bands that's held every year, and Rodrick thinks if Löded Diper works hard to get ready, they can actually WIN it.

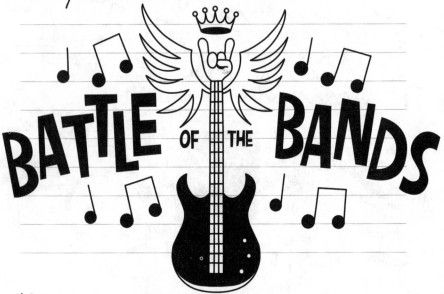

Rodrick's favorite band, Metallichihuahua, won the Battle of the Bands when they were just starting out.

I'm not a big fan of that kind of music, and the only reason I've even heard of Metallichihuahua is because Rodrick's bedroom is plastered with their posters.

Rodrick says the Battle of the Bands competition launched Metallichihuahua's career, and afterward they were on the cover of every magazine.

12

Metallichihuahua broke up before Rodrick got a chance to see them play, so everything he knows about them is from magazine articles and old concert footage. But when Bill was ten years old, his gramma took him to see Metallichihuahua on their last tour. And he's always bragging about it to Rodrick.

In fact, sometimes Bill still wears the T-shirt he got from that concert, even though he probably SHOULDN'T.

I have no idea if it's realistic for Löded Diper to win this competition or not.

But if Rodrick's band actually goes on to fame and fortune, I'M gonna be the one to tell their story. Because if I have to suffer through Löded Diper's band practices, I figure I might as well get something out of it.

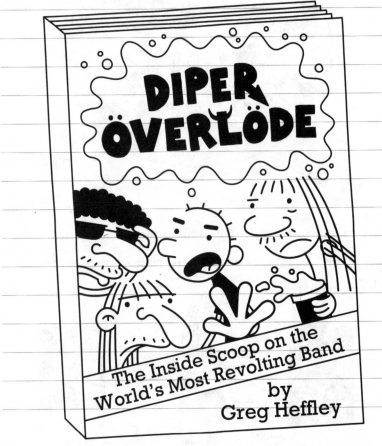

DIPER ÖVERLÖDE

The Inside Scoop on the World's Most Revolting Band
by
Greg Heffley

Wednesday

Rodrick told his bandmates that one of the reasons
Metallichihuahua got people to take them seriously
early on was because whenever they were out in
public, they looked like they were already famous.

He said the first step in making people think you're
a rock star is to DRESS like one.

So the other night the guys went to the mall to buy
some cool outfits. But they found out that trendy
clothes are really expensive, and that ripped jeans
cost twice as much as brand-new ones. So they left
without buying anything.

They came back to our house and ripped their OWN jeans. But when Mom found them piled up in Rodrick's room, she put patches on the holes. And I'm pretty sure she IRONED them, too.

After that, the guys went to the Goodwill store, where you can get used clothes pretty cheap. And Bill put together an outfit that he thought made him look like the lead singer of a rock band.

But it turned out that half the clothes Bill bought had been donated to the store by his gramma, so she made him turn right around and return them.

Then Mackie had an idea. He said they could just buy rock star COSTUMES, because the Halloween outlet near us was having an after-season clearance sale. And everybody agreed that seemed like a smart plan.

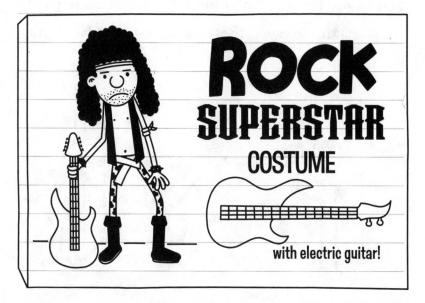

ROCK
SUPERSTAR
COSTUME

with electric guitar!

But the costumes didn't look anything like they did on the packaging. They were more like plastic aprons than cool outfits, and the guitars were miniature inflatables.

If the guys ever go out in public wearing those plastic aprons, I really hope Bill wears some pants underneath. Because those costumes only cover the FRONT.

Thursday

Rodrick says that every serious band gets professional photos taken so they can use them on posters and album covers. But it turns out professional photographers are EXPENSIVE, so Rodrick's been looking into other options.

The option he settled on was asking Mom to take the pictures, because she offered to do it for free. So they spent the afternoon doing a photo shoot in our backyard.

But it was hard to get a shot where there wasn't a fence or a swing set in the background.

19

After a while they ditched their costumes and just tried using the stuff around them. But they ended up with a bunch of pictures they're probably not gonna use.

Mom said the guys looked too serious in all the pictures, and music was supposed to be FUN.

So she got them to lighten up a little. But I
don't think the guys are gonna like the way those
photos came out, either.

Eventually it got too cold out and the guys moved
inside. Mom had other things to do, so I got put
on photographer duty.

Rodrick wanted to get a few photos that would really tell people what Löded Diper is all about, which is how we ended up in the bathroom.

But Drew and Mackie started screwing around, and Drew ended up with a toilet plunger stuck to his back. The guys were about to go to the emergency room, but then Rodrick remembered that one of our neighbors is a plumber.

After that, the guys looked through all the photos, but they didn't think they looked professional enough.

Mackie remembered that there was a photo studio at the mall that could probably do this kind of thing pretty cheap. Everybody liked that idea, so they piled into Rodrick's van and headed to the mall.

But what Mackie forgot was that the photography place at the mall was a BABY studio.

I guess the studio isn't choosy about whose pictures they take, though, and they had the guys in front of the camera in no time.

It took a little while for them to warm up to the photographer, but apparently this lady was really good at making her subjects feel comfortable.

The session lasted an hour, and the photographer took a TON of pictures. But I don't see any of those photos making their way onto Löded Diper's posters, either.

I guess the guys still wanted their pictures, though. It was cheaper to order a calendar than to buy individual photos, so that's the package they went with. Mom's already using it as our family calendar, so I guess that means we've got twelve months of Löded Diper to look forward to.

<u>Sunday</u>

Rodrick thinks the only way for Löded Diper to win the Battle of the Bands competition is to play a bunch of shows and keep improving. But right now they don't have a good way of getting around.

A few weeks back, Rodrick's van got rear-ended by someone, and now he can't open the back doors. That means it's practically impossible to load all the band's equipment into the van.

Rodrick looked into getting the doors replaced, but he found out it would cost more to get new ones than the van is actually WORTH.

But then the guys saw an ad for a contest that a local car dealership was having called "Hands on a Van," where the person who can keep at least one hand on a brand-new van the longest gets to KEEP it. So they decided this was the answer to their transportation problems.

Rodrick and the other guys spent a lot of time debating which one of them should enter the contest to win that van. But Mackie said that if they ALL entered the competition, they'd have four times the chances of winning it.

The contest started on Friday night. I think the guys were planning on this thing lasting a few hours, and when it was over, they'd drive off in their new van. But that's not how it played out.

When they got to the dealership, there was a huge crowd. And even though the contest hadn't officially started, people were already in position.

HANDS ON A VAN

Once the competition got going, the rule was that if you took your hand off the van for even a second, you'd be OUT.

That meant there were no potty breaks. And thirty minutes into the competition, Drew was really wishing he hadn't just downed a sixty-four-ounce soda.

Drew was the first person to drop out, but a long time went by before anyone else did. And three hours later, everyone was still going strong.

A lot of contestants had packed coolers with food, because they must've known they were in for a long night.

But Rodrick and the other guys weren't prepared, so Rodrick called Mom and asked her to bring them sandwiches.

Mom was too busy to drive down to the dealership, so she sent me on my bike. And when I got there I handed the guys their food.

Bill was paranoid that he was gonna accidentally take his hand off the van, so he kept BOTH hands on the vehicle. And that meant I had to feed him, which was kind of awkward.

I stuck around for a little while, but it was pretty boring watching a bunch of people standing there doing nothing, so I went home. But in the morning, Rodrick's van wasn't in the garage, which meant he was still at the dealership.

Mom sent me back down there with bagels and orange juice. And even though a lot of contestants had quit overnight, there was a handful of people still in it. But some of them looked like they were ready to crack.

A few contestants started playing mind games to psych each other out. One lady began singing really loud and out of tune, and some old guy opened up a can of what smelled like expired tuna.

Another guy started reading the phone book from the beginning to annoy everyone else.

And I guess that was too much for Mackie, because he lost his nerve before the guy even got through the Bs.

It was pretty clear that sleep deprivation was taking its toll on everyone. And one lady got eliminated for trying to pet a dog that wasn't even THERE.

A few hours later, there were only a few people left. Bill and Rodrick seemed like they might fall over at any second, and they were up against a lady who looked like she could easily go another two DAYS. And I think the guys were seriously considering giving up at that point.

But the lady was watching some game show on her TV, and when she got a question right she lost her focus just long enough to get eliminated.

I thought that was the end of the contest, but it wasn't, because Bill and Rodrick got into an argument over which one of them should actually win the van.

Rodrick said it should be him, because all the band equipment was at his house. But Bill said it should be HIM, because he'd never had his own vehicle before.

And those two guys are more stubborn than I realized, because neither one of them budged for two whole hours.

Around ten o'clock that night, Rodrick came up with a compromise. He said that they could SHARE the vehicle, and whenever the band didn't need the van for a show, Bill could use it.

Bill said he was OK with that, so they took their hands off the van at the same time and shook on it.

But they probably should've checked to make sure no one was on the other side of the vehicle before they let go. Because I'm pretty sure the guy who ended up winning was only a few minutes away from throwing in the towel himself.

Tuesday

After the Hands on a Van contest, Rodrick and his bandmates realized they weren't gonna be playing shows any time soon. So they've been brainstorming OTHER ways to get their music out there.

They decided what they needed to do was post a bunch of stuff on social media and build a following that way. So they created an account and started posting clips of them playing music in our basement.

LD @LodedDiper4REAL
posted two photos

Those first posts didn't get many views, so they decided to change things up by filming in more interesting places. But those videos didn't take off, either.

Then, the other day, Bill dropped a speaker on his foot, and Mackie was filming when it happened.

They posted that video as a joke, and it was their most popular one yet.

Then they started posting a lot MORE stuff like that, and their channel REALLY took off.

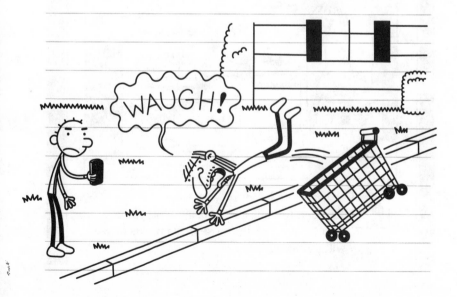

But after a few trips to the emergency room, the guys realized things had gotten out of control. And even though they had a ton of "likes," they weren't getting their music out there, which was the whole point to begin with.

So the guys went back to just posting clips of them playing music, and they lost a ton of followers. And after a while they even gave THAT up because it wasn't worth the hassle.

40

Wednesday

Rodrick decided that Löded Diper should forget about filming clips for social media and focus on making a real music video instead.

So the guys have been watching all of Metallichihuahua's early videos, and they decided their best one was for the song "Dog Eat Dog," which they filmed at a kennel with real Chihuahuas.

Metallichihuahua   "Dog Eat Dog"

The reason that video is so famous is because nobody fed the dogs before the shoot started. And as soon as they opened the cages, the dogs went after the lead guitarist, who was snacking on a ham and cheese sandwich.

Rodrick and the guys spent a lot of time talking about what they could do in their own music video to TOP Metallichihuahua.

Drew said maybe they could shoot a video in the sewers, but they couldn't figure out how to get Rodrick's drums down the manhole. Mackie suggested they film their song "Monkey House" in a real monkey house at the zoo, but they were a little worried the monkeys might act up.

Then Bill said they should do a video where they parachuted out of a plane. And Rodrick liked that idea because he said it would get people's attention.

But Mackie has a fear of heights, so he vetoed that one.

Drew said that maybe they could do what Metallichihuahua did for their "Dog Eat Dog" video, only with BABIES.

And everyone seemed to like that idea because they couldn't remember anyone doing something like it before.

But it turns out you can't just borrow a bunch of babies for a few hours, or at least you can't in the state where we live.

The guys realized they were getting a little ahead
of themselves anyway, because they needed to
record a SONG before they could start thinking
about making a music video to go along with it.

Löded Diper has recorded some of their music
before, but they've never actually used professional
equipment to do it.

Last year, they taped a bunch of stuff on Manny's
toy tape recorder, but I guess the playback
quality isn't great on those things.

And anyway, Mom erased everything they recorded after she got a call from the teacher at Manny's preschool.

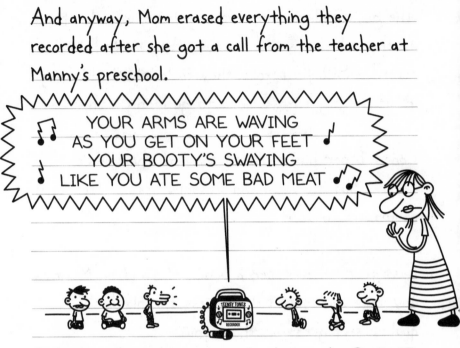

♪♫ YOUR ARMS ARE WAVING
AS YOU GET ON YOUR FEET ♪
YOUR BOOTY'S SWAYING
LIKE YOU ATE SOME BAD MEAT ♫

Rodrick said it was time to do things the RIGHT way and record their music in a real studio. But just like everything else, those types of places cost a lot of money.

So Bill asked his gramma if he could be a few months late with the rent, which gave the guys just enough money to pay for some time in a recording studio. And even though they only needed one song to make a music video, they decided to record enough songs for a whole ALBUM.

Rodrick says that when Metallichihuahua was big, bands used to put out albums with cool artwork on the record covers. And he's got a few of their best albums on the wall above his bed.

Rodrick says that nowadays, people don't appreciate album art because they just download music on their phones.

His plan is to release Löded Diper's first album as a vinyl record so the art can be really BIG.

Rodrick and his bandmates went to a recording studio downtown today, and I decided to tag along.

There was one room where the engineer had a bunch of computers, and another room with lots of instruments and microphones.

I guess the guys were pretty excited about all the different instruments, because as soon as they saw them they had to play every one.

Eventually, Rodrick said it was time for them to get serious. I thought they'd start recording songs right away, but they hadn't even decided which ones to put on their album yet. And if you ask me, they probably should've figured that out BEFORE they got to the studio.

It turns out Löded Diper has over fifty songs, and they spent a lot of time trying to whittle it down to the ten they wanted to record.

And I have no idea what made them choose some songs over others, because from the titles, it felt like they were all about the same kind of stuff.

SONGS

One-Wiper

Can You Smell Us Now?

Diper Överlöde

~~Exploded Diper~~

Diper Igniter

Potty Mouth

~~Leaky Kamode~~

Down the Drain

Monkey House

~~The Runs~~

Raise a Stink

Smell Test

Stink It Up

~~Toilet Lips~~

~~Bloated Diper~~

Rodrick thought they should have at least one
track with swear words in it because that way you
get a Parental Warning sticker on your album.
And he said if you DON'T have one of those
stickers, teenagers won't buy it.

**PARENTAL
WARNING**
OFFENSIVE LYRICS

But Mackie said he didn't want to have any songs
with swear words because he wanted to make an
album his mom could enjoy. So Rodrick said if they
were making music for Mackie's mom, then they
might as well just quit right now.

Then things got pretty heated between the two of them, and it took a long time for them to cool down after they were separated.

Once that situation was under control, the guys debated which song they should record first. Bill thought it should be "Can You Smell Us Now?" because he likes the line that goes "We're leakin' through your speakers like a chocolate cow."

But Drew said that line didn't even make sense because there's no such thing as a chocolate cow. So Bill went after Drew and then THOSE two had to be separated.

Rodrick decided the song should be "Diper Överlöde," which was the first one he ever wrote. And I guess the other guys were tired of fighting because they agreed.

But it didn't take long for a NEW problem to crop up. While Drew and Bill were arguing about song lyrics, Mackie accidentally dropped his pick into the hole in the middle of an acoustic guitar.

So then the guys took turns trying to get the pick back out. And I can't even tell you how much time THAT took.

RATTLE
RATTLE

Eventually, Drew managed to shake the pick free, but it went straight down Bill's THROAT.

And it was kind of scary for a minute there.

Luckily, Mackie knew some sort of maneuver to get the pick dislodged from Bill's throat. All I can say is that I'm glad there was a window between the engineer's booth and the room where the band was.

Bill was badly shaken up, and he said he wanted some time to recover. But Rodrick said they really needed to get going if they wanted to record a whole album.

So everyone picked up their instruments and got in their places, and the engineer hit "record." Rodrick played the drum intro to "Diper Överlöde," and then Mackie and Drew started in with their guitars.

But Bill only made it through two or three verses before he had to stop, because apparently that guitar pick really did a number on his throat.

Somebody got Bill a bottle of water, and a few minutes later he was good to go. And the second time around they managed to get all the way through the song without Bill choking.

AND YOU AIN'T BEEN THIS COVERED SINCE THE LAST TIME IT SNOWED!

After that, Rodrick and his bandmates were feeling pretty confident, and they were ready to rip through the rest of their songs. But the engineer said they'd have to come back and do it another day because their time was up.

So I guess if they want to finish their album, Bill's gonna have to ask his gramma for a few more months of credit on his rent.

Saturday

The guys were pretty bummed they wasted so much time at the studio the other day, but they were glad they got that one song down. Because that meant they could make a music video, which was their goal to begin with.

They didn't have any money to produce their own video, but what they DID have was a gift certificate that Mackie's little sister never ended up using.

57

But it turns out Shooting Stars Studio doesn't do videos for original songs.

They have a menu of songs you have to choose from. And I don't think the guys were all that thrilled with the selection.

VIDEOS

Best Friend	Late 4 School
Gossip	Cute New Boy
Puppy Love	Beach Day

Bill wanted to do the song about gossip, but Rodrick wanted to do the one about being late for school because it sounded the most rock 'n' roll. But Mackie said he got to make the decision because it was his sister's gift certificate.

And even though I doubt they'll ever show the video they made to anyone, it looked like they had a lot of fun doing it.

Löded Diper   "Beach Day"

Wednesday

The guys were disappointed that they didn't get to make a music video they could use, but they realized that they still had a song, and there was a lot they could do with that.

They figured if they could get a radio station to play "Diper Överlöde," then that would be even BETTER than posting a music video online.

So they took their song to a bunch of local radio stations. But most of the places they visited said it wasn't a "good fit" for their listeners.

They probably should've done a better job researching some of the stations they visited, though, because it would've saved them a lot of time driving around.

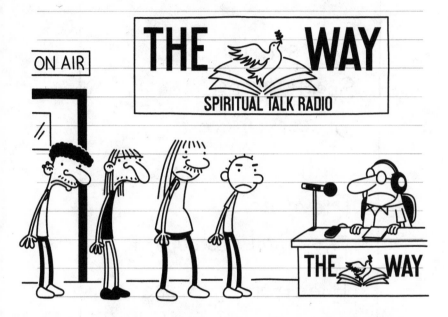

Rodrick said the problem wasn't that their song was bad, it was that the people who choose what to put on the radio have terrible taste in music.

So he decided that if they wanted to get their music heard, they were just gonna have to get CREATIVE.

Rodrick said there are a LOT of places that play songs besides radio stations, so they made a list of everywhere they've ever heard music in public.

Gas station
Sports arena
Grocery store
Mall
Elevator
Fast-food restaurant
Electronics store
Dentist's office

The guys spent a few days working the phones, trying to track down the people who make the decisions on these kinds of things. But they just hit a bunch of dead ends, so they drove around town to try and find the right people to talk to.

But that didn't get them anywhere, either.

After that, they started talking to people they actually KNEW. But nobody was willing to play their song.

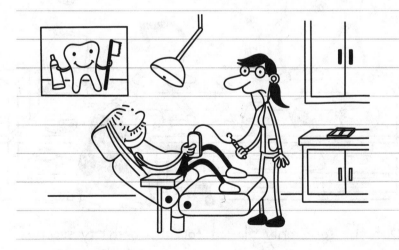

Then they had a breakthrough. Drew's older brother worked at the deli counter at the grocery store, and he had access to the sound system in the back office. So the guys finally got to hear their music in public for the first time.

YES IT'S A DIPER
A DIPER ÖVERLÖDE
AND YOU AIN'T BEEN THIS COVERED
SINCE THE LAST TIME IT SNOWED

But the song only played for about thirty seconds before the deli manager shut it off.

And I guess he wasn't a fan of that kind of music, because he fired Drew's brother before his shift was even over.

The guys were pretty frustrated they couldn't get anyone to play their song, but then Bill said maybe they needed to take a different approach.

He said TV commercials usually have music in them, and maybe they could convince some company to use Löded Diper's music for one of their ads.

Bill said if they were lucky, they might even get their pictures on some packaging. But Rodrick said that once Metallichihuahua started going down that road, it was the beginning of the end for them.

But I bet if Bill could get his face on some packaging, he'd jump at the chance.

Tuesday

Last week, Löded Diper finally caught a lucky
break. When Rodrick went down to the junkyard to
see if he could find some doors to replace the ones
on his van, he found a replacement VEHICLE.

Somebody had abandoned an old ice cream truck
at the junkyard, and the guy who owned the
place told Rodrick he could have it for free if he
could get it off the lot. And even though the
truck was rusted, it still ran.

The guys were excited, because there's plenty of
room inside the truck for all their band equipment.
And this means they can actually start doing
SHOWS again.

But the thing they were most excited about was the speaker on top of the vehicle. And when Rodrick brought the truck home, the guys spent the weekend cruising around town blasting their music.

After they got tired of that, they started calling different clubs to find someone who would hire them to do a show. But it's been a long time since Löded Diper actually played anywhere, and none of the places they called had even HEARD of them.

So Rodrick and the guys have been trying to think of ways to get themselves noticed.

The other night they drove around playing their music from the roof of their ice cream truck. But they didn't get past the elementary school, which recently installed speed bumps in the drop-off zone.

Rodrick said that if Löded Diper really wanted to make a splash, they were gonna have to start thinking a lot BIGGER.

He said that when Metallichihuahua was starting out, they played a concert from the rooftop of a building in the middle of the city, and it caused a huge scene.

The police and fire departments shut them down, but by the time they did, Metallichihuahua was already all over the news.

The band got fined for disturbing the peace, and even spent the night in jail. Then they used their mug shots on the cover of their first album.

Rodrick's big idea was to do a show from the top of the same building Metallichihuahua played on thirty years ago. Mackie wasn't crazy about the idea, though, because he said that getting arrested wouldn't look good on his college applications.

But Rodrick said that the minute they saw the police coming, they'd take off. And I guess Mackie wanted to be a team player, because he agreed to go along with it.

So this afternoon the guys packed up the ice cream truck with all their equipment and drove downtown.

Their plan was to use the elevator to get to the roof. But security's gotten a lot tighter since that rooftop concert, so Rodrick and his bandmates didn't even get past the lobby.

The guys weren't ready to give up, though, so they parked in an alleyway and waited by a side door until someone came out. Then they started making their way up the stairwell with their equipment.

But that turned out to be a lot harder than they thought it would be.

Bill wanted to turn around and find a building that didn't have so many floors. But Rodrick said they were already committed and they just needed to keep going.

After taking lots of breaks between floors, they finally got up onto the rooftop. Then they set up all their equipment, but couldn't find any electrical outlets for their speakers and guitars.

So Rodrick tried to get the lady who lived in the apartment one floor below to let them use her outlet.

The guys thought the lady was gonna call the cops, and they all got spooked. So they gathered up their gear and went back down the stairwell.

It should've been easier going down than coming up, but they were in a rush, so their getaway didn't go that smoothly.

As soon as the guys made it back out to the alley with all their gear, they started loading it into the ice cream truck.

That's when a police cruiser drove up and blocked them in.

The guys started freaking out because they thought they were about to get arrested for trespassing. But it turns out the cop didn't even know they'd been up on the roof.

The police officer told them they were parked in a loading zone, which comes with a fifty-dollar fine.

But I guess she felt sorry for them because she let them off with just a warning.

PARKING VIOLATION	
Blocking a loading zone	$50
☑ WARNING (fee waived)	

And even though Löded Diper didn't get the publicity they were hoping for, they're already talking about using their run-in with the law for their first album cover.

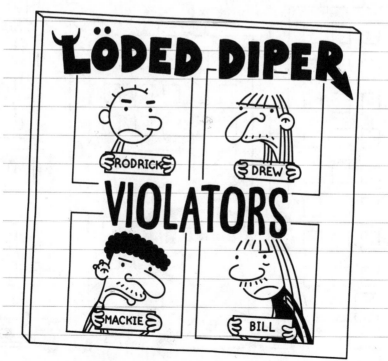

<u>Sunday</u>
The rooftop concert didn't go the way they planned, but the guys started dreaming up new stunts to call attention to themselves. And some of their ideas were pretty crazy.

Bill's idea was to drop a thousand-pound diaper from the top of a skyscraper. But nobody knew where they could get a diaper that big, and none of them wanted to climb all those stairs again anyway.

Drew said maybe they could do the same thing with a REGULAR-size diaper from a lower floor, but the other guys agreed that wouldn't have the same effect.

PIFF

Then Rodrick came up with a plan that was REALLY nuts. He said that if they put diapers on all the statues in the city park in the middle of the night, people would want to know who was responsible. And then when Löded Diper announced they were the ones behind the stunt, they'd be famous.

So they bought three dozen diapers and drove down to the city. But I guess the park has someone watching it twenty-four hours a day, and they got busted.

After that, none of the guys had the stomach for another big stunt.

So they decided to play it safe and just get some stickers made with the band's name on it.

Today the guys spread out and put the stickers up all over town. And they must've burned through half their supply in public bathrooms alone.

After they were done, Rodrick called up a few of the clubs that said they'd never heard of them to see if they knew who they were NOW. And the owner of Renegades Rock Club told them he knew exactly who Löded Diper was and that they should come downtown for a meeting.

The guys were pretty excited, because Renegades is one of the best places for live music. But it turns out they had stickered the owner's SUV, so they spent the rest of the afternoon scraping them off his vehicle.

Saturday

I guess those stickers weren't a waste of money after all.

The club next door to Renegades is called the Headless Chicken, and the other day the owner reached out to Rodrick to invite the band downtown to talk about playing a show.

She said the Headless Chicken has live music every Thursday night, and if Löded Diper wanted to play there, she'd give them half of the admission she charged at the door.

The guys couldn't believe they actually lined up a paying gig, and they spent all week getting ready for the show. Since they were gonna be playing on an actual stage, they wanted to make sure their setup looked really cool. So Mackie made a giant Löded Diper banner to hang behind the band, and Rodrick got a fog machine from the Halloween store.

Bill wanted to get one of those laser projectors to really put things over the top. But Drew's convinced those things are DANGEROUS, so they had to scrap that idea.

Rodrick wanted to make his drum set look extra cool for the show, so he came up with the idea of putting skulls on the tops of his cymbals.

I thought he was gonna pick up a few plastic skulls at the Halloween store, but he was only interested in the real thing. And I guess people aren't just handing those things out to anyone who asks.

Rodrick said a show isn't just about the music, it's about the whole experience. He said they could turn the fog machine into a SMELL machine and have a different odor for each song. But when Mom found out about that idea she shut it down because she said it was "unsanitary."

The guys had a lot of OTHER plans for their stage set, but most of them were too expensive or just unrealistic. But then Bill came up with an idea that seemed like it might actually work.

He said they could buy one of those plastic porta-potties, and when it was time for the band to go out onstage, they'd all come out of it for their big entrance.

So they started calling around to find a place that sold porta-potties, and found out those things cost a lot of money when they're brand new.

Drew's uncle ran a construction site, and he was willing to sell the band a used porta-potty at half price. So the guys went to pick it up today.

But I guess loading that thing into the truck took a lot out of them. And now they're worried about getting the porta-potty and all their equipment onstage Thursday night and still having enough energy to perform.

So the band has been trying to find someone who can help move the equipment in and out of the truck on Thursday night.

Rodrick asked his friend Ward first, because he used to work security for the band at their shows. But Ward wasn't willing to help out unless they made him a full member of the band.

Then Drew asked his brother if he'd do it. But he was still sore over getting fired from his job at the deli counter, and he said he'd only take the gig if they paid him the money he would've got at work.

I guess the guys were out of options, which is why they came to ME.

Rodrick said they couldn't pay me anything, but the experience would look great on my resume. I don't know what kind of employer would be impressed that I worked for a band with the word "Diper" in its name, though.

But I figure taking the job will make my Löded Diper tell-all book a lot more interesting. So really, I'm just in this for the DIRT.

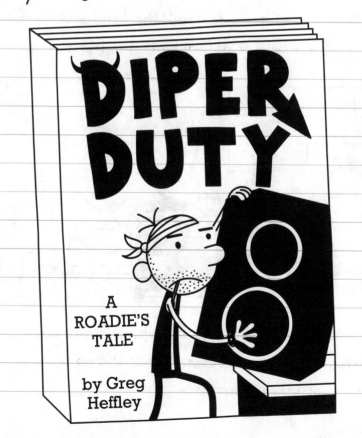

DIPER DUTY

A ROADIE'S TALE

by Greg Heffley

Saturday

If every night is like Thursday night, I'm not sure how long I can SURVIVE being Löded Diper's roadie.

The band wasn't supposed to go onstage at the Headless Chicken until 8:00, but Rodrick was pretty anxious to get everything set up. So we got there two hours ahead of time and started hauling the gear inside, and the band was happy to let the new guy do most of the grunt work.

It took over an hour to set up, and the guys wanted to squeeze in some rehearsal time before the crowd started arriving.

But then Rodrick realized he forgot his drumsticks at home. And he blamed it on ME, because he said that roadies are responsible for the equipment.

There wasn't enough time to go home and get back by showtime, so Mackie started calling around to see if any stores in the area had drumsticks. But I guess the only music store in town closed a few months ago, so that was a dead end.

Then Rodrick had an idea. He said there was a Hipp 'O' Henry's a few blocks away, and we could get drumsticks THERE. But that didn't make a lot of sense to me, because Hipp 'O' Henry's is a pizza place.

Rodrick reminded me that every Hipp 'O' Henry's has a robot band that comes out three times a night to play a song. And even though it's been a while since I've gone to one of those places, I remember being kind of freaked out by those robots when I was younger.

Rodrick's idea was to somehow grab the drumsticks, which sounded a lot like STEALING to me. But Rodrick said we wouldn't be stealing, we'd just be BORROWING them for a few hours. And he said we'd probably have the drumsticks back before anyone even noticed they were gone.

I didn't like the sound of that, but it turns out Rodrick couldn't pull this plan off WITHOUT me.

Hipp 'O' Henry's doesn't allow teenagers in their restaurants, because I guess they've caused a lot of trouble in the past. So Rodrick's plan was to have me go in with Bill and pretend he was my FATHER.

This whole thing seemed like a terrible idea to me, but I guess I felt a little responsible for leaving those drumsticks at home, so I went along with the plan.

NO UNACCOMPAN MINORS

Me and Bill walked past the security guard into the restaurant. But it felt like that guy knew we were up to something because he didn't take his eyes off us once we were inside.

So Bill got some tokens and did his best to act like he really was my dad when I got a good score playing Whac-A-Mole.

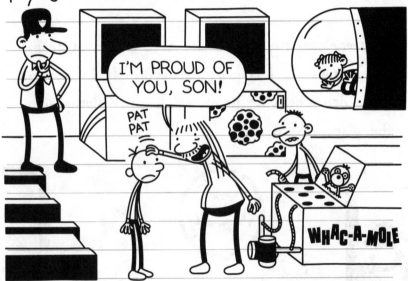

Me and Bill played Skee-Ball, and things got pretty competitive between us. And I guess we got kind of carried away, because by the time we were through, Bill must've spent at least twenty bucks on tokens.

We took the tickets we earned to the prize counter, and Bill was disappointed we couldn't afford the lava lamp. So he spent another ten dollars in tokens to play a few more rounds of Skee-Ball, and we won enough tickets to put us over the top.

All that activity made us work up an appetite, so we sat down to order some pizza. And I'll admit, I was having so much fun that I forgot the reason we were there in the first place.

But when the curtains opened and the robot band started playing, I remembered what we came to do.

The robot monkey started playing the drums, but it wasn't like we could just go up onstage and take the drumsticks out of his paws with everyone watching. So we just sat there and tried to figure out how we were gonna pull this off.

But before we could come up with anything good, the curtains closed, and everyone just went back to eating their pizza.

I still had no idea how we were gonna get those drumsticks, but then one of the customers created the distraction we needed.

Some kid's mom started complaining to the manager about her pizza. She said the slices were different sizes and had different toppings on them, which meant that the restaurant was using leftover slices and selling them as NEW pizzas.

I remembered my mom complaining about the same thing a few years ago, which is the reason she stopped taking us to Hipp 'O' Henry's.

With everybody's attention focused on this lady's conversation with the manager, me and Bill made our move. We slipped behind the curtains and went backstage, where it was pitch-black.

Bill turned the flashlight on his phone on so we could see, and the robots were as still as statues in the dark.

I knew those things weren't actually ALIVE, but I definitely didn't feel comfortable being around them. So I wanted to hurry up and get this over with.

But it wasn't that easy. We tried to get the drumsticks out of the monkey's paws, but he had a death grip on those things.

And I don't know if the robots were motion-activated or WHAT, but when the monkey opened his eyes, it totally freaked me out.

I decided to bail on the mission, and I went out the back door. Bill was right behind me, but he didn't come out empty-handed.

Luckily, the other guys had pulled around to the back in the getaway vehicle. And that side window definitely came in handy.

SCREECH
TOSS

We thought we were in the clear after we got out of the parking lot, but the security guard was right on our tail in his Hipp 'O' Mobile.

REEEEEEEEE

He chased us through traffic, and Rodrick couldn't shake him. Then we hit a red light and the security guard stopped his vehicle and approached the truck on foot.

When the light turned green, Rodrick hit the gas and left the security guard in our dust.

SCREECH

Mackie was totally freaking out because he said we could go to jail for resisting arrest. Rodrick said a security guard at Hipp 'O' Henry's couldn't actually put someone under arrest.

Rodrick wasn't taking any chances, though. He took a few quick turns and then pulled the truck around the back of a Chinese restaurant. Then he cut the engine and the lights, and we waited it out until we were sure the coast was clear.

Mackie wanted to go back to Hipp 'O' Henry's and return the monkey paw. But Rodrick said there was no time for that, because Löded Diper was supposed to be onstage at the Headless Chicken any minute.

So he drove across town and parked the truck in the alleyway behind the club, then we went in through the back door. The manager was waiting for us inside, and she told the guys they needed to hurry up and get onstage because the crowd was starting to get restless.

The problem was that we only had one drumstick, and that was still in the monkey's paw. And none of the guys could figure out how to pry it loose.

Then Drew had an idea. He connected a speaker wire to one of the wires dangling from the monkey paw, and when he did, the paw opened and let go of the drumstick.

But when Drew disconnected the wires, the paw closed again. And this time it clamped shut on Mackie's LEG.

That's when the club owner came backstage and told the guys that if they didn't get out there and start playing, she'd never hire them to play at the Headless Chicken again.

And even though Mackie was having trouble walking with a giant robot monkey paw attached to his leg, he managed to get onstage with the rest of the band.

The crowd seemed like they were in the mood to be entertained, but Löded Diper wasn't ready for their big moment.

First of all, the guys all seemed pretty shook up
by that car chase, so nobody was at their best.
Rodrick was only working with one drumstick, and
Mackie was more focused on the monkey paw than
on his guitar playing.

On top of that, they all just seemed kind of
rusty since they hadn't performed in front of a
crowd in a while. But the person who was the most
out of practice was BILL. He couldn't remember
any of the words to the songs, so he had to read
the lyrics off his phone.

106

And from all the squinting he was doing up there, I'm guessing he might be due for reading glasses.

Bill probably should've put his phone on airplane mode before the show started, because then it wouldn't have rung when his gramma called. But I guess Bill doesn't like to keep his gramma waiting, because he answered his phone in the middle of a song.

The crowd was starting to get annoyed, and they let the band know it by pelting them with chicken wings.

But I was dealing with a BIGGER issue. People started lining up to use the porta-potty, and I couldn't do anything to STOP them.

Thankfully, the club ran out of chicken wings, and the audience started to head home. And that was a good thing, because Bill got Buffalo sauce in his eye and couldn't read the lyrics off his phone anymore.

Once everybody was gone, we started breaking down the set. But the lady who owned the place made us pick up all the chicken wings and clean the sauce off the stage, which added another hour to our night.

SCRAPE

SCRUB
SCRUB

SWISH

After the equipment was loaded into the truck, Rodrick asked the owner about getting paid. There was a pretty big crowd in the club, and Rodrick was expecting Löded Diper to walk away with a decent amount of cash.

But the club owner said the deal was that the band would get half the money she charged for admission at the door, and on Thursday nights she lets people in for FREE. That means the whole thing was just a scheme to sell chicken wings.

So after all that trouble, the guys didn't get anything out of it, unless you count a robot monkey paw. And don't even ask me how Mackie explained that thing to his teachers at school the next morning.

Wednesday

After the way Löded Diper performed at their last show, it seems to me like they should be spending a lot more time practicing. But they've been spending all their free time trying to get this monkey paw off Mackie's leg instead.

Drew said maybe they could try the thing with the wires again, but Mackie's worried that could make the monkey paw squeeze even TIGHTER and totally crush his leg. Mackie wants to bring the paw back to Hipp 'O' Henry's, because he thinks if he reconnects the paw with the robot monkey, it'll set him free.

SHINKT

HºH

But Rodrick says the security guard is probably waiting for them to show up again, and that's the LAST place they should go. So the guys have been searching the Internet to find someone who handles this sort of thing. But so far they haven't had any luck.

What's kind of crazy is that Metallichihuahua used to have a giant robot dog as a part of their stage show, which they brought out during the encore.

The robot dog had glowing red eyes and it shot steam out of its nose. And during the band's last tour, their bass guitarist got too close to one of the giant Chihuahua's nostrils and paid the price for it.

The guys got curious about what happened to that guitarist, whose name is Warwick Sprinter. So they looked him up to see what he's doing these days.

It turns out Warwick is still kicking, and he even has a website where you can book him for private events and stuff.

ROCK LEGEND
Warwick Sprinter

APPEARANCES · MERCHANDISE · PRIVATE EVENTS

PRIVATE EVENTS

Rock icon Warwick Sprinter is available for private events at surprisingly affordable rates!

Book Warwick for your next:
- Corporate event
- Bachelorette party
- Company retreat
- Baby shower
- Sweet Sixteen

Sometimes he does public appearances where people can meet him. And when the guys checked his calendar, they found out he was scheduled to be at the Legends of Yesteryear convention, which is this weekend.

I've actually been to that convention with my dad. He was a fan of some fantasy show that used to be on TV when he was a kid, and when he found out some of the actors were gonna be there signing autographs, he wanted to go and meet them.

But the people who show up at these things really get into it, and I actually felt a little weird being one of the only people there not wearing some kind of costume.

Legends of YESTERYEAR

MAIN HALL

CELEB ROW

Dad was a little disappointed that the main stars of his show weren't there, but he was still pretty happy to meet some of the second-tier actors.

I guess a lot of these actors make their living off events like this, so Dad shelled out a lot of money on autographed photos and memorabilia while we were there.

It's not just actors who go to these things, though. There were retired athletes and washed-up rock stars at the Legends of Yesteryear convention when I went with Dad, but they weren't getting much traffic at their tables.

TEDDY BROCK

Ricki Stallion

THERESA STAMPS

It must be hard to go from performing in front of thousands of people to sitting at a plastic folding table by yourself in a convention center. So the whole thing made me feel kind of SAD.

But Rodrick and the guys are totally fired up about this thing. Because the way they see it, they're finally gonna meet a real LEGEND.

<u>Saturday</u>

Rodrick and the guys brought a ton of stuff
to get autographed by Warwick Sprinter at the
Legends of Yesteryear convention. But it turns out
they weren't allowed to bring items from home, so
the guys had to put them all back in the truck.

Once they got inside, they went to look for
Warwick's table, and they found him in the back.

Rodrick and his bandmates were so excited to meet Warwick that they started talking over each other. But his rule was that if you wanted to ask a question, you had to BUY something first. And he had a whole tableful of expensive stuff to choose from.

But the guys didn't have a ton of cash, so Rodrick bought the cheapest item, which was a Metallichihuahua eraser. Then he asked Warwick what advice he had for a band that was trying to break into the music business.

Warwick said the most important thing is to never do anything for FREE.

He said a lot of people will try to take advantage of a group that's just starting off, but a band should always make sure they get paid for their work. And after what happened at the Headless Chicken, that seemed like pretty good advice.

Rodrick wanted to ask another question, but first he had to buy something else. So Rodrick and the guys pooled the rest of their money and bought a Metallichihuahua candy dispenser.

Rodrick asked what made Metallichihuahua break up all those years ago. And Warwick had a lot to say on that subject.

He said there were two reasons the band broke up: MONEY and EGO. He said things were going great for Metallichihuahua until they found out their manager had been stealing from them. And after they fired him, they needed to figure out a way to replace the money he stole.

That's when they started making bad business decisions and signed a bunch of endorsement deals just to make a quick buck.

MINTY LICKS
CANINE TOOTHPASTE

He said they created a bunch of products they weren't really proud of, including a line of personal fragrances that ended up on the bargain shelf two weeks after it came out.

But Warwick said the worst decision they made was to create a Saturday morning cartoon show for little kids, because it turned off their older fans.

He said things got really bad for the band when people started whispering in their lead singer's ear and telling him he was the REAL star of Metallichihuahua, and he didn't need the other guys. So he made a solo holiday album, which totally flopped.

Warwick said after that, things fell apart for the band. Metallichihuahua tried to make money touring with a new singer, but fans had moved on. And a few years later, they decided to just call it quits.

He said that after the band broke up, everyone went their separate ways. The original singer went back to school and eventually became a lawyer, and the lead guitarist went into some kind of law enforcement.

Warwick said that nobody has heard from the band's drummer, Sebastian Sleeves, in twenty-five years. Then Warwick pulled out a magazine with Sebastian's last interview in it, and said he'd be willing to unload it for twenty-five bucks.

DOG GONE!
METALLICHIHUAHUA'S SEBASTIAN SLEEVES HANGS UP HIS COLLAR

They say every dog has his day, and Metallichihuahua's drummer, Sebastian Sleeves, is clearly having his. Interviewed in his newly built mansion, complete with a pool with twin Chihuahua fountains, Sleeves is reflecting on his legacy with Metallichihuahua and where his path might take him next.

Sebastian Sleeves relaxes in his expansive pool.

But the guys were out of cash. So Warwick told them there was an ATM right down the hall, and that he'd be happy to wait for them.

Then Warwick said he had a whole garage full of Metallichihuahua merchandise he's been trying to get rid of, and if they wanted to swing by his place sometime, he'd be happy to give them a really good deal on some quality items.

But I guess Rodrick and the guys were a little uncomfortable, and they felt like they already got everything they came for. And even though Rodrick told Warwick they were gonna hit that ATM and come back, they went straight home instead.

Thursday

The one good thing that came from Löded Diper meeting that guitarist is they've decided that from now on, they're not doing anything without getting PAID.

Mom said there are plenty of people who need a live band for their events, so the guys have been trying to get the word out that they're available for weddings and other stuff.

But advertising in the newspaper is expensive, so they've been putting ads in the church bulletin instead.

St. Martha's Parish Bulletin

Today's service celebrates the life of Edward M. Row, who is survived by his wife, Edna, and their daughters, Marleigh and Alice.

CHURCH RAFFLE
Win a chance to have a bouncy house for your child's next birthday party. Tickets are $5 each.

BAND FOR HIRE
Löded Diper will perform at your next event. Cash payments only. Fees negotiable. If interested, talk to Rodrick Heffley's mom after today's service.

YOUTH GROUP
Next meeting to be held in rec hall due to basement flooding.

That hasn't gotten them any bites, so the guys started asking their friends if anyone needed to hire a band. It turns out one of Mackie's friends has a cousin who was having a bar mitzvah. And I guess his parents were pretty desperate for entertainment, because they offered to hire Löded Diper without even asking to hear their music.

The guys were pretty excited they finally booked a paying gig, but then Mom told them that a bar mitzvah is a formal event and they were gonna have to dress up for it. But they solved that problem with a trip back to the Halloween store.

SECRET AGENT COSTUME

WITH BOW TIE!

Rodrick told me they were gonna need my help setting up for the event, but I decided my days of working for free were over, too. So I told him if he wanted me to keep working for them, I was gonna need a 10% cut of whatever the band got paid from now on, which he agreed to.

I'd never been to a bar mitzvah before, so I didn't know what to expect. But the food was great and the whole thing was a lot of FUN.

Everyone was having a great time, and when Löded Diper stepped onstage, the party kicked up a notch. And nobody even seemed to mind that the band's lyrics weren't really appropriate for a religious celebration.

WE'RE COMIN' THROUGH YOUR SPEAKERS
RUNNIN' THROUGH YOUR TOWN
WE'RE POURIN' THROUGH YOUR HEADPHONES
AND YOUR EYES ARE TURNIN' BROWN.

When Löded Diper took a break, the kid whose party it was opened his gifts, which were mostly books and stuff like that. But then his parents surprised all the OTHER guests with gifts, too.

Each person got their own Nerf gun and a hundred suction-cup darts. And from that point on, it was just a free-for-all.

THWOCK

Everybody had a blast, and at the end of the party, the kid's parents paid the band in cash. And I got my 10%, just like Rodrick promised.

I guess word got around that the band did a good job, and within a few days, Löded Diper had a string of gigs lined up.

They did a boat show, a fundraiser for injured firefighters, and even a contest that judged the ugliest dog in the state. And Bill actually got to pick the winner of that one.

After that they played a lumberjack competition and the grand opening of a tattoo parlor.

But the wildest event they did was for a baby formula company that was throwing a party for new moms. And I couldn't tell if those women actually liked Löded Diper's music or if they were just excited to get the chance to blow off some steam.

Bill, Drew, and Mackie were happy with the way things were going because they were finally making some money. But the person who didn't seem satisfied was RODRICK.

He said it was great to have some extra spending money, but if they wanted to win the Battle of the Bands, they needed to get serious about growing their fan base.

He said that when Metallichihuahua was starting out, they used to play shows seven nights a week, and they had a group of fans who followed them from place to place to see them perform.

Rodrick said Metallichihuahua's fans called themselves the Bone Brigade, and they dressed up in crazy outfits for shows.

Rodrick thinks that if Löded Diper wants to win the Battle of the Bands, they're gonna have to get crazy fans of their OWN.

He said that they could get one of those T-shirt guns and shoot diapers into the crowd at their shows.

The other guys weren't crazy about that idea because now that they had a little money, they didn't want to spend it all on diapers.

But Rodrick had already thought that through. He said that if they could find a SPONSOR, then they could get diapers for FREE.

And believe it or not, he actually booked a few meetings with baby supply stores and pitched his idea. But none of them seemed all that enthusiastic about having their brand connected with a heavy metal band.

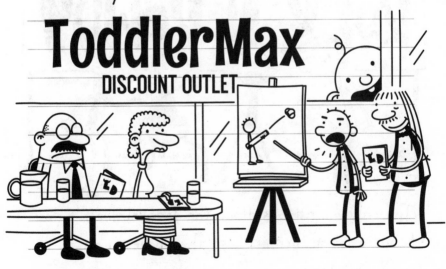

Saturday

I guess all those events Rodrick's band booked weren't such a waste of time after all, because now a lot more people know who Löded Diper is. And today they got invited to play at a music festival that's happening a few weeks from now.

The Rock 'n' Rowdy festival is an outdoor event where a bunch of bands play in front of tons of people. And the guys are all excited because they've been going to that thing as fans for YEARS.

The only downside is that the festival doesn't pay bands a lot to perform, so they have to make money in other ways.

And the way Löded Diper is planning on making money is by selling a lot of MERCHANDISE.

Rodrick says that every band that performs at the Rock 'n' Rowdy festival has a merch table in the parking lot. But he says they've got a leg up on the competition because of their ice cream truck.

The problem is that the band doesn't actually HAVE any merchandise yet, and there's not a lot of time to create any. So they've been scrambling to figure out what they can actually get made in the next three weeks.

Drew wants to create bobbleheads, and says they can make one for each band member.

But Mackie's all about the PLUSH, because he thinks it would be cool to have a beanbag doll of himself.

138

Bill thinks plush is too YOUNG, so he wants to make a comforter set for the older fans instead.

Rodrick said that when Metallichihuahua was at its peak, they had their own toothbrushes with bristles that were made from the band's actual hair.

But I guess Bill is worried about losing his own hair, so he didn't seem all that crazy about the idea.

The thing that got the guys the most excited was creating their own line of energy drinks. And they even came up with a name for their product.

Rodrick said maybe they could put a drop of sweat from each band member in every can.

But Mackie said something like that would never get past the Food and Drug Administration.

Once they started researching how you actually got
stuff made, they found out it was too expensive
and there wasn't enough time, anyway. So they
decided to just use their leftover stickers and slap
them on things that were lying around our house.

But I can't imagine who's gonna buy a used Löded
Diper iron at a music festival.

Rodrick isn't just relying on merchandise sales to
make extra money, though.

He says that some bands have a "meet and greet"
after their shows, where hard-core fans can pay
to hang out with the group.

Rodrick says that some people are willing to spend big bucks just to get an autograph and a picture.

So the guys spent a few hours tonight coming up with meet-and-greet packages at different price levels.

LÖDED DIPER
Meet 'n' Greet
PACKAGES*

Wave Hello $2

High Five $5

Handshake $8

Selfie $10

Autograph Item . . $15

* Prices are per band member

Mackie thought they should have something for a Löded Diper "superfan" who was willing to drop a bundle for a more exclusive experience. And that's how they came up with the Full Diper.

FULL DIPER

Includes every Meet 'n' Greet item

★ PLUS ★

- ☑ Photo with whole band
- ☑ Ten-minute conversation
- ☑ Share the band's snacks
- ☑ Hold Rodrick's drumsticks
- ☑ Half-hour singing lesson with Bill

$70

But as someone who's already spent a lot of time with the band, I can tell you firsthand that there are better ways to spend your money.

Sunday
Rodrick and his bandmates wanted to get to the
festival a few hours before they were scheduled
to perform so they could sell merchandise in the
parking lot. But I guess fans like to arrive at
these things really early, because by the time we
got there, all the good spots were already taken.

The guys found a space for the truck next to the
porta-potties, which wasn't the greatest place to
sell merchandise.

And the only reason they sold anything at ALL was because people were desperate for toilet paper.

An hour before it was time for Löded Diper to perform, we unloaded all the equipment from the truck and hauled our gear to the main stage.

But it turns out Löded Diper wasn't scheduled to be on the main stage, which was a big disappointment for the guys. They were performing on the SMALLER stage, which was on the other side of the festival grounds.

There wasn't a lot of time before the band was scheduled to go on, so we got there as fast as we could. But there was no need to rush, because there weren't all that many fans to see Löded Diper anyway. And there was at least one person who looked like he didn't even want to be there.

Even though the guys were disappointed in the number of people who showed up, Rodrick still wanted to get diapers out into the crowd. So he put me in charge of that.

But we only had a few and never did manage to get
our hands on one of those T-shirt guns.

Once the set was done, the guys wanted to just
pack up and go home. But unfortunately, Mom
signed up for the Full Diper, so we were stuck
there for a while.

<u>Friday</u>
After the Rock 'n' Rowdy Fest, none of the guys seem that motivated to practice. The Battle of the Bands is just a few weeks away, but I think they all know they don't have a realistic chance of WINNING it.

Rodrick decided the only thing that can turn things around for Löded Diper is a pep talk from someone who's been in their shoes. He thinks if they can track down Metallichihuahua's drummer, Sebastian Sleeves, that guy could give the band the spark it needs.

Sebastian Sleeves is basically Rodrick's hero, and he's always talking about how great he is.

148

According to Rodrick, one time Sebastian burned his hands in a hamburger-grilling accident, and it looked like Metallichihuahua was gonna have to cancel its world tour.

But Sebastian taught himself to drum with his FEET, so the band didn't even miss a show. And from then on he just kept doing it that way.

The only problem in finding this guy is that it doesn't seem like he wants to be found. Because after he did that last magazine interview, he basically dropped off the face of the earth, and nobody's heard from him since.

But Rodrick's made it his mission to find Sebastian Sleeves. So lately Rodrick's been going through old magazine articles and pictures to see if he can find any clues that might give a hint about where Sebastian is NOW.

Rodrick's hit a bunch of dead ends, but last night Mackie had a genius idea. He said that if you build a pool, you have to get a PERMIT, which is part of the public record.

The guys started looking up all the pool permits that were issued around the time that last picture of Sebastian was taken. And even though there were a lot of pools built that year, there was only ONE in the shape of a Chihuahua head.

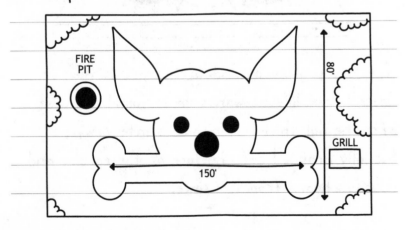

FIRE
PIT

GRILL

80'

150'

The guys looked up a satellite image of the property, and there was a big wall around it. So it seemed like just the type of place a rock star would live.

They all agreed that when they got to the house, they couldn't just drive up to the front gate and ring the doorbell. Drew said maybe they could scale the walls and sneak onto the property. But famous people always have lots of security, so that seemed like a TERRIBLE plan to me.

Bill said that maybe they could just wait for Sebastian to come outside the gate, and they could toss him inside the truck. But none of the guys were sure if that was actually LEGAL.

They couldn't agree on a plan, so they just agreed to wing it when they got there.

I usually like to tag along with the band, but I decided to sit this one out. Because even though I knew whatever happened would probably make a good chapter in my book, it didn't seem like it was worth going to JAIL over.

Saturday

I'm glad I trusted my instincts for once, because when Rodrick filled me in on everything that happened today, I was happy I didn't have to experience it firsthand.

The band left early this morning, and when they got to the property, they knew they had the right place.

They sat there for a while trying to figure out what to do. But while they were arguing over their next move, a food delivery person pulled up to the gate, dropped off a bag, and drove away.

A minute later, the gate opened, and there was Sebastian Sleeves in the flesh. Only he looked twenty-five years older than he did in the picture in the magazine.

Rodrick stepped out of the ice cream truck, and when he did, Sebastian spotted him. And I guess this wasn't the FIRST time Metallichihuahua fans had shown up at his house, because he was back inside the gate before the guys got within ten feet of him.

Sebastian walked away, but Rodrick yelled and asked him to stop. Rodrick said they weren't there for autographs, and that they just wanted to TALK.

Sebastian must've been willing to hear what Rodrick had to say, because he stood there while he ate his burger.

Rodrick told Sebastian that they were all huge fans of Metallichihuahua and they were trying to follow in their footsteps. And he asked if Sebastian had any advice on how Löded Diper could make it to the top.

Sebastian took a minute to finish his burger and fries, then he pressed a button and opened the gate. And none of them could believe what was happening.

They followed Sebastian onto the property, and even though the mansion was still pretty impressive, it looked like it had seen better days.

Sebastian stopped at the pool, which was barely recognizable from the picture in the magazine. Then he handed the guys some cleaning supplies.

He said he'd be happy to talk as long as they cleaned the pool. So the guys got to work while Sebastian drank his soda on the diving board.

Sebastian told the guys that when the band ran out of money, he had to sell off all his expensive cars and fancy things just to pay the property taxes. And when he burned through THAT money, the state shut off his water and electricity.

So he's been living off the tiny royalty checks that come in from the "Metallichihuahua Pups" show, which apparently still runs in Denmark.

But Rodrick wasn't really interested in hearing this guy's sob story, so he tried to change the subject by asking him what advice he had for Löded Diper.

I think Rodrick was hoping Sebastian would give them a pep talk, but he gave them the OPPOSITE. He said that nowadays there's no place on the radio for a band that writes their own songs and plays their own music.

So if Löded Diper REALLY wanted to make it big, he said they needed to ditch their instruments, learn how to lip-synch, and hire a choreographer.

Then Sebastian said it's practically impossible to make it in the music business anyway, so the best advice he could give the guys was to quit now and focus on their education instead.

Because if they didn't, they might end up like him, flat broke and living in a pool house with no electricity or running water.

I guess it was a long ride back for the guys, and when they got to our house, nobody was in a talkative mood. And all anyone wanted to do was go home to take a shower and wash off the smell of pool chemicals.

<u>Tuesday</u>

After their trip to see that drummer, Rodrick and the guys were down in the dumps. The stuff Sebastian said really rattled them, and they even talked about taking his advice and calling it quits.

It probably would've been a relief for Mackie, whose grades are in the toilet because of the band. Drew was thinking about taking his brother's old job at the deli counter, and Bill was talking about how nice it would be to have a little more free time to spend with his gramma.

But for Rodrick, quitting wasn't an option. He said they shouldn't listen to what some washed-up rocker had to say, because that guy was just bitter things hadn't worked out for HIM.

Rodrick said the reason Metallichihuahua broke up was because they became everything they used to be AGAINST. And he said as long as Löded Diper sticks together, nothing can stand in their way.

I guess the other guys were inspired by Rodrick's speech, because suddenly they were all in. Bill said Löded Diper could become more popular than Metallichihuahua EVER was, and maybe even become the biggest band of all TIME.

Mackie said if they wanted to be the biggest band of all time, they were gonna have to do something nobody's ever done before.

So Drew said maybe they could play a concert in outer space, which all the guys were pretty excited about, even though none of them seemed to have any idea how that would actually WORK.

GASP!

SPUTTER!

Bill said Löded Diper could have a ride at an amusement park, and he even threw out a few concepts that everyone liked.

But Rodrick said Bill was thinking too SMALL. He said Löded Diper should have their own theme park, and the guys even sketched out a map of where everything would go.

Mackie said they'd make so much money from their theme park that they could afford to destroy their instruments at the end of every show, just like Metallichihuahua used to do.

But then Bill had an even CRAZIER idea. He said they should build a giant robot baby that would come out during the last song, and when the concert was over, it would destroy the whole set. And everybody thought that was the best idea YET.

Then Drew said the baby could double as the band's transportation, and they could use it to get around.

Even though the guys were pretty excited about their ideas, the giant robot baby will have to wait until they save up a little money. So for now they're gonna have to settle for what they could get at the Halloween store.

CRYING BABY MASK

Saturday

Ever since Löded Diper decided to stick together, they've been laser-focused on getting ready for the Battle of the Bands. But it turns out they've got a little COMPETITION.

There's a new band that's been putting their posters up all over town. And it looks like these guys have a lot in common with Löded Diper.

Rodrick and the other guys are pretty ticked off, because they think Stank is nothing but a Löded Diper rip-off. They even stole Löded Diper's idea with the stickers.

But what's REALLY annoying Rodrick is that it looks like Stank got themselves a sponsor, and one of their billboards is right above our highway exit.

It's not just Stank's posters and billboards that are everywhere. It's their MUSIC, too. And it feels like you can't go anywhere without hearing one of their songs.

They've already got a huge social media following, and they've got an army of fans called "Stankers," who seem pretty passionate about the band.

Rodrick's nervous that Stank is gonna steal Löded Diper's thunder at the Battle of the Bands, so he decided they should go to a Stank show to see how big of a threat they are.

But Rodrick didn't want anyone at the show to recognize them, so he decided they should go in DISGUISE. Unfortunately, by now all the good costumes at the Halloween store were gone, so they had to settle for the leftovers.

I think the guys were hoping Stank would live up to their name, but apparently they were actually really GOOD. They played a two-hour set without taking a break, and they kept their energy up the whole time.

The fans knew the words to all their songs, and Rodrick got mad when Bill joined in.

PEOPLE, CAN YOU SNIFF OUR DRIFT?
🎵 JUST SNIFF A LITTLE WHIFF! 🎵

Stank even had a smell machine, which they cranked up when they played their big hit, "Sniff a Little Whiff." And from the way Rodrick's clothes smelled when he came home tonight, I'm guessing they loaded the machine with rotten eggs.

It sounded like things couldn't have gone much WORSE for Löded Diper. And the only person who had a good time was Bill, who walked out of the show with a bunch of Stank gear.

Saturday

Now that Rodrick knows who Löded Diper is up
against in the Battle of the Bands, he's more
focused than EVER.

He says if Löded Diper wants to beat a band like
Stank, they're gonna have to OUTWORK them.
So he's been holding practice twice a day, once in
the morning and once at night.

But I think the new schedule is really taking a
toll on Bill, who's been stealing quick naps during
Mackie's guitar solos.

Rodrick's been riding Bill harder than anyone, though. He said if Löded Diper's gonna win, they're gonna have to really bring the energy during the competition. So he put Bill on a diet and exercise program to help whip him into shape.

But Rodrick found out Bill was cheating on his new diet plan when he discovered a stack of empty donut boxes in the back of the ice cream truck.

When Rodrick confronted Bill about the donuts, Bill confessed that he started going to Huneybuns every morning before band practice. He said he started going there for the coffee and donuts, but the reason he's been going back is because he's in LOVE.

Here's how Bill said it happened. A few weeks ago, Bill stopped by Huneybuns, but when he pulled up to the pickup window, the ice cream truck got stuck under the overhang.

It was raining that day and Bill didn't want to get wet by stepping out of the passenger door.

So he decided to crawl out of the truck through the pickup window. And that's where he came face-to-face with the assistant manager, Becky, for the first time.

According to Bill, it was love at first sight, and they've been dating ever since. Then Bill said he didn't think he could keep doing two practices a day because Becky gets off her shift at 6:00 p.m. and he wants to be able to hang out with her in the evenings.

Rodrick said the band needs all the rehearsal time it can get, and that Bill could start inviting Becky to evening practices so the two of them could be together.

But I think Rodrick regretted it right away,
even though Becky always brings a few boxes of
leftover donuts to practice.

The first few times Becky came to practice, she
didn't say a whole lot. But now she's starting
to get a little more comfortable, and she's been
making lots of suggestions for how Löded Diper
could do things differently.

Becky thinks Löded Diper has too many songs
about body smells and toilets, and most girls aren't
really into that sort of thing. So she said the
band should think about making their songs a
little more female-friendly.

She even took one of the songs that Rodrick wrote and marked up the lyrics.

Can You ~~Smell~~ Hear Us Now?

Can you ~~smell~~ hear us now?
You're ~~sweatin' indigestion~~ listenin' to music
and ~~your stomach's in knots~~
you're movin' your feet

Can you ~~smell~~ hear us now?
You ~~better check your~~ can't believe your eardrums
~~underwear~~
'Cause ~~I'm seein' spots~~
this music is sweet

Can you ~~smell~~ hear us now?
We're filling up your ~~nostrils~~ headphones
And you're ~~moppin' your brow~~
noddin' your head

178

Then Bill started writing his OWN songs. And most of them were ballads to his new girlfriend.

> I ORDERED AT THE DRIVE-THRU
> AND I NEVER ASKED YOUR NAME
> BUT THEN I SAW YOUR NAME TAG
> AND I'LL NEVER BE THE SAME
> OHHHH, BECKY
> YOU SET MY HEART AFLAME

This morning, Rodrick told Bill Löded Diper doesn't do slow songs, and the romantic stuff was gonna have to GO. But Bill said Rodrick was just jealous because he's never been in love and he doesn't know what it's like.

Bill wasn't finished, either. He said Becky's been telling him that since he's the lead singer, he's the face of the band. And she even created a new poster with Bill front and center.

But I guess that was too much for Rodrick to take. He said he was the one who started Löded Diper, and if anyone was gonna be the face of the band, it was gonna be HIM.

Then Rodrick said since he was the leader of Löded Diper, that meant he got to call the shots. He told Bill that his relationship with Becky was a big distraction, so the new rule was that nobody was allowed to date until the competition was over.

Bill wasn't happy about it, but I guess he felt like he didn't have much choice, so he agreed to put his relationship with Becky on hold. The only problem was that he was too chicken to tell her himself, so somehow that fell to ME.

And I hope I never have to break up with anyone in person again, because I've gotta say, it's not a whole lot of FUN.

<u>Monday</u>

Things haven't been good with the band since
Rodrick and Bill had their big blowup.

Bill realized he made a mistake splitting up
with Becky, and the next day he tried to get
her BACK. But she stopped taking his calls and
now she won't even take his coffee orders at the
donut shop.

So now Bill's totally heartbroken, and he's been
skipping practices.

And even when he DOES show up, he can't get
through a song without breaking down in tears.

> YOU'RE MY DIPER IGNITER
> YOU LIT ME WITH YOUR LIGHTER
> AND NOW THE FLAME IS GROWIN'
> AND IT'S ONLY GETTIN' BRIGHTER

SOB
SOB
SOB

Rodrick hasn't exactly shown Bill a lot of
sympathy. He says that Bill has got to pull himself
together if Löded Diper is gonna win the Battle
of the Bands. But it seems like the competition is
the LAST thing on Bill's mind.

So Bill's mad at Rodrick, and the other guys
in the band have kind of had it with him, too.
Mackie's getting tired of the two-a-day practices,
and Drew's mad because he really liked getting
those free donuts from Becky.

Right in the middle of their big fight, Mom came downstairs with a letter that was addressed to Rodrick.

And from the first page, it looked pretty OFFICIAL.

TAYLOR & FISCH Attorneys at Law

VIA CERTIFIED MAIL
Stewart Taylor, Jr., Esq.
Taylor and Fisch
The Clark Building
400 Canal Street

CEASE AND DESIST

The letter was from a lawyer who says he represents a company that used to publish a line of trading cards called the Revolting Runts.

I guess those trading cards were super popular back when my parents were kids, and the characters definitely lived up to their name.

The reason the lawyer sent the letter was because one of the Revolting Runts characters was called "Loaded Diaper," and apparently it was one of their most popular cards.

REVOLTING RUNTS

LD

LOADED DIAPER

The lawyer said that even though the Revolting Runts went out of print a long time ago, the company still owns the trademark to the characters. And he said that if Löded Diper doesn't change its name, the company is gonna sue the band for "monetary damages."

After Rodrick finished reading the letter out loud, the other guys seemed kind of shaken up. But Rodrick said he wasn't gonna change Löded Diper's name because of some stupid letter, and if they stayed strong, they could FIGHT this thing.

But none of the other guys had the stomach for an expensive legal fight, and they seemed happy to let Rodrick deal with this one on his OWN.

SCREECH

Friday

I never would've guessed that a trading card company would be the thing to break up Löded Diper, but it looks like that's exactly what's happened.

Ever since Rodrick got that letter, the other guys have steered clear of our house. So with the Battle of the Bands just a week away, Rodrick's been trying to recruit new band members to fill the empty slots.

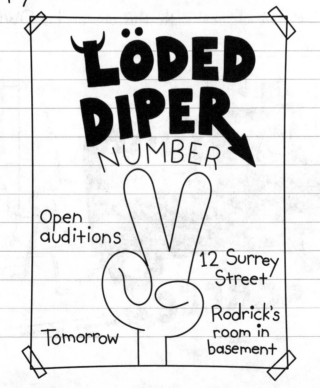

LÖDED DIPER NUMBER

Open auditions

12 Surrey Street

Tomorrow

Rodrick's room in basement

But nobody even showed up for the first round
of auditions, so Rodrick put up a NEW flyer
promising free pizza to anyone who tried out.

And even though the new ad got people to come
to the house, it seemed like it drew a lot more
pizza lovers than actual musicians.

A handful of people who showed up had some
musical talent, but none of them were a good
fit for Löded Diper's style of music. And unless
Rodrick's gonna start writing songs that feature
harmonicas and glockenspiels, he's probably gonna
have to keep looking.

But the slot Rodrick was MOST worried about
filling was the lead singer position, because there
aren't a lot of people out there who can hit the
high notes on "Explöded Diper" and the low ones
on "Down the Drain."

Löded Diper's not the ONLY band looking for a
new lead singer, though.

Word got around that the lead singer of Stank blew out his vocal cords during one of their shows, so now they're scrambling to find a replacement, too.

And from their flyers, it looks like they're willing to offer people a lot more than a few slices of pizza to come out and audition.

<u>Wednesday</u>

Well, it didn't take long for Stank to find their new lead singer. And I guess I shouldn't have been too surprised by who it was.

The only thing that DID surprise me was what they had to do to get their guy. Because from the look of their new poster, I'm guessing Bill and Becky came as a packaged deal.

Now that Bill is a member of Stank, Rodrick is even more obsessed with winning the competition. And I think he'd do just about anything to walk away with first prize.

The problem is, he still hasn't found anyone to take the place of his old band members. So he's moved on to plan B, which unfortunately involves ME.

Well, not JUST me. Drew's brother and Rodrick's friend Ward are part of the plan, too. Even though none of us have any musical talent, Rodrick thinks he can train us to play "Diper Överlöde" in time for the competition. But three days into rehearsals, it's not looking so good.

Rodrick says that in a rock 'n' roll band, it's 20% talent and 80% ATTITUDE. So he's been trying to teach the three of us how to look like we belong onstage.

Mom even bought us outfits for the show, which I guarantee none of us will be wearing.

So at this point I'm praying Rodrick comes up with a plan C and that I'm not a part of it.

Saturday

When I woke up this morning, the first thing I remembered was that it was the day of the Battle of the Bands.

I had already decided I didn't want to be involved, and my goal was to be as far away as possible when the competition started. But Rodrick must've sensed that I was gonna get cold feet, and he wouldn't let me squirm out of it.

Drew's brother and Ward got to our house just after lunch to help load up Rodrick's van with equipment. But I really wished Rodrick had gotten those back doors fixed, because it was no fun getting everything into the vehicle.

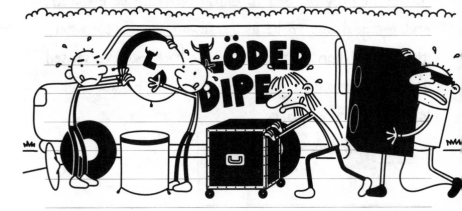

On our way to the arena, I had a sick feeling in my stomach. I could barely play two chords on the guitar, and Ward couldn't remember half the words to "Diper Överlöde." And I guess Drew's brother was nervous about the whole thing, too, because he had to breathe into a paper bag to keep himself from passing out.

But Rodrick told us we'd be fine once we got out onstage, and we just needed to TRUST him.

196

By then we were pulling up to the arena, and there was no turning back.

People were selling merchandise in the concourse, and Stank had a big table set up near the entrance. And somehow Becky had managed to get bobbleheads made in time for the event.

But Becky wasn't the only familiar face inside the arena. Warwick Sprinter had a table there, too, but it didn't seem like his stuff was selling.

We were looking for the backstage entrance when Rodrick spotted someone ELSE we'd seen before. And I don't know what the Hipp 'O' Henry's security guard was doing so far from the restaurant, but it didn't seem like a good idea to go up to him and ASK.

We finally found our way backstage, which was a total ZOO. Most of the bands were already there, and the space was way too small for everyone.

Stank walked in a few minutes before the competition started. And they really lived up to their name, because they smelled like they hadn't had a shower in WEEKS.

WAVE
WAVE

I could tell Rodrick wanted to go up to Bill and SAY something, but he was swarmed by music journalists, so Rodrick couldn't get close to him. And it was pretty clear Bill was saving his voice for his big performance, anyway.

POINT POINT

There was a screen in one corner of the room that listed all the bands in order of when they were scheduled to perform.

And I was pretty disappointed that Löded Diper was dead last, because all I wanted to do at that point was get this over with and go HOME.

But Löded Diper wasn't the only band that was performing at the end of the competition. Stank was scheduled to go on right BEFORE us.

That meant we had to hang out with Bill and his new bandmates backstage, which was really awkward. So when the competition started, I decided to slip out the side door and watch the show from the wings.

There were at least a thousand people in the audience, which made me feel queasy all over again. And they were already getting rowdy before the competition even STARTED.

When the first band came onstage, the crowd went totally NUTS. And they didn't let up for the rest of the night.

All the bands sounded the same to me, but the audience didn't seem to mind. Everybody was there to have a good time, including the security guard from Hipp 'O' Henry's, who I guess was just there as a fan.

The bands were all WAY more professional than Löded Diper, and I'm guessing most of these groups did this full-time. So I could tell that we were out of our league in this competition.

I thought about making a run for it to save myself the embarrassment of having to perform. But at that point it didn't seem right to ditch Rodrick.

I knew the time for Löded Diper to go up there was getting close when Stank took the stage. I thought they'd come out and tear into one of their big hits, because that would've definitely made the crowd go wild. But Bill came out by himself and sat down at a piano.

And when he started playing a slow song, the crowd didn't seem to know how to react.

I SAW YOU THERE
LOOKIN' OH SO SWEET
WITH YOUR COLLARED SHIRT
AND YOUR PANTS PRESSED NEAT

But it was all just a big fake-out, because then the rest of the band stepped onstage and launched into a speed metal version of "Becky."

OH BECKY, YOU FILL ME UP SO HOW 'BOUT YOU POUR ME ANOTHER CUP?

The audience was totally eating it up, and I knew right then that Stank had this competition in the bag. And that was BEFORE Becky started tossing donuts into the audience.

TOSS

STANK

Huneybuns

I should've been a little more careful about how close I was to the crowd, though, because the next thing I knew I was PART of it.

I guess I kind of let myself get swept up in the moment, because for a second there I forgot I was supposed to be onstage NEXT. But when I saw Rodrick at the stage door, I remembered why I was there.

PSST!

We had a minute to get ready backstage, so me and the other two guys tried to talk Rodrick into just accepting defeat and letting Stank win the competition.

But Rodrick was too stubborn to go down without a fight. So when the announcer called Löded Diper's name, the three of us followed Rodrick out onstage.

The stage lights were so bright that I couldn't see past the first three rows of the audience. But I locked eyes with the guy from Hipp 'O' Henry's, and I could tell he recognized me.

I wanted to RUN, but I felt trapped up there. And when Rodrick started playing the drum intro to "Diper Överlöde," I knew I just had to grit my teeth and get through the next three minutes.

But then something WEIRD happened. When I started playing the guitar chords Rodrick taught me, I sounded WAY better than I did during practice. And Drew's brother had somehow gotten a lot better, too.

But when Ward opened his mouth to sing, it was BILL'S voice that came out of the speakers. And suddenly it all made sense.

Rodrick had plugged his music player into the sound system, and what was coming through the speakers was the version of "Diper Överlöde" the guys recorded in that studio back in December.

That meant me and Drew's brother were only PRETENDING to play, and Ward was just lip-synching to Bill's vocals.

And once Ward realized he didn't have to sing for REAL, he started to actually enjoy himself.

Nobody in the crowd seemed to notice that we were faking it, and I guess I started to have a little bit of fun, too.

I couldn't really blame Rodrick for using a prerecorded track for the competition, because even if we had three MONTHS to practice, we never could've pulled it off.

So everything was going great, and I thought we might actually have a shot at winning the whole thing. But then it all came crashing down.

Halfway through the song, Bill stopped singing and started COUGHING. And Ward didn't know what to do, so he just tried to keep up as best he could.

That's when I realized that Rodrick had
accidentally played the first version of the song
they recorded, right after Bill got a guitar pick
stuck in his windpipe.

But it was too late to switch over to the GOOD
version of the song. And when the sound of Bill
drinking water came through the speakers, the
crowd finally noticed something was off.

It seemed like a good time to get out of there.
But we couldn't leave the stage because someone
was standing in our WAY.

It was some guy wearing a suit and holding a manila envelope, which he handed to Rodrick.

It turns out this guy was the lawyer from that trading card company, and he was there to officially deliver Rodrick the news that his company was taking Löded Diper to COURT.

But then things got a whole lot WEIRDER, because the Hipp 'O' Henry's security guard was suddenly onstage, and closing in FAST.

I just froze, because I didn't know if this guy was gonna arrest me or WHAT.

But the security guard blew right past me and walked up to the lawyer, then started arguing with him about something. And a few seconds later, Sebastian Sleeves climbed out of the crowd to join in the conversation.

GRUNT WHEEZE

I had NO idea what was going on. But when Warwick Sprinter appeared from backstage and started going at it with the other three, I finally put it all together.

The four guys standing onstage were the original members of Metallichihuahua.

And I guess they had a lot of things they needed to get off their chests, because it got really heated up there.

But then the crowd realized what they were witnessing, which was the first Metallichihuahua reunion in twenty-five years. And everybody started going BANANAS.

I think all the cheering took the members of Metallichihuahua off guard, because they stopped talking. And when the cheers got even LOUDER, the ex-bandmates knew what they had to do.

So they grabbed our instruments and totally blew the ROOF off the place.

Metallichihuahua ripped through their greatest hits, and then they played an encore. And the only reason they didn't play a SECOND encore is because they had already smashed our instruments to bits.

Thursday

So Metallichihuahua became the first band to ever win Battle of the Bands TWICE. The competition vaulted them back to the top of the charts, and they're even planning a world tour.

I heard that Drew took his brother's old job at the deli counter, and that Mackie got accepted to a school for robotics. So maybe he'll finally figure out how to get that monkey paw off his leg.

After the competition, Stank didn't need Bill anymore, so they fired him. But luckily Löded Diper was in the market for a lead singer, so I guess it worked out for everyone.

It looks like it might be a while before my services are needed again, which is totally fine with ME. Because I've definitely had my fill of the rock 'n' roll lifestyle.

ACKNOWLEDGMENTS

Thanks to my brother, Scott, for sharing your hilarious stories and insight about the rock 'n' roll lifestyle.

Thanks as always to Julie for your invaluable support. I couldn't do this without you!

Thanks to Charlie Kochman for your encouragement and support in helping me make these books the best they can be. Thanks to Mary O'Mara for the steadiness and skill you bring to this process. Special thanks to Steve Roman.

Thanks to the Wimpy Kid team—Shaelyn Germain, Vanessa Jedrej, Anna Cesary, and Colleen Regan—for making work so much fun!

Thanks to everyone at Abrams, especially Michael Jacobs, Andrew Smith, Elisa Gonzalez, Hallie Patterson, Melanie Chang, Kim Lauber, Alison Gervais, Erin Vandeveer, and Borana Greku.

Thanks to the wonderful team at An Unlikely Story and to Rich Carr, Andrea Lucey, Paul Sennott, Sylvie Rabineau, and Keith Fleer.

Thanks to everyone at Disney, especially Roland Poindexter, Michael Musgrave, Kathryn Jones, Ralph Milero, and Vanessa Morrison.

Thanks to Jess Brallier for helping me launch my career!

ABOUT THE AUTHOR

Jeff Kinney is a #1 *New York Times* bestselling author and a six-time Nickelodeon Kids' Choice Award winner for Favorite Book. Jeff has been named one of *Time* magazine's 100 Most Influential People in the World. He spent his childhood in the Washington, D.C., area and moved to New England, where he and his wife own a bookstore named An Unlikely Story.